Ebbé finds his Heart

Ebbé finds his Heart

Written by

Susan Kauer-Ritchie

ARCHWAY PUBLISHING

Archway Publishing books may be ordered through booksellers or by contacting:

Archway Publishing
1663 Liberty Drive
Bloomington, IN 47403
www.archwaypublishing.com
1 (888) 242-5904

Because of the dynamic nature of the Internet, any web addresses or links contained in this book may have changed since publication and may no longer be valid. The views expressed in this work are solely those of the author and do not necessarily reflect the views of the publisher, and the publisher hereby disclaims any responsibility for them.

Any people depicted in stock imagery provided by Thinkstock are models, and such images are being used for illustrative purposes only. Certain stock imagery © Thinkstock.

ISBN: 978-1-4808-2765-3 (sc)
ISBN: 978-1-4808-2766-0 (e)

Library of Congress Control Number: 2016902045

Print information available on the last page.

Archway Publishing rev. date: 2/11/2016

The spring morning yawned cold air on Ebbé's back. He pulled the blanket up around his shoulders, mad at himself for bringing only one. He was cold and sore from sleeping on the hard ground. The journey had been just a few short weeks, but his body and spirit felt old beyond his years.

Ebbé had passed through his youngling years and was beginning his early middle years. He was of average height for a troll, about two feet in hand measurements, but shorter than his younger brother. His brother was forever teasing him, saying he was cut from serious cloth, which in part was true. He had, though, inherited his father's perpetual smile and twinkling eyes, which offset the part of him that pondered the world and its ways.

And this was the why of his journey.

Ebbé stood up and stretched as he wrapped his blanket around his shoulders. Picking up his knapsack, he wondered what this new day would bring. "Uff da. Now which way to go? I wish I had a clue," Ebbé said, looking out at the forest that stretched around him like a dark green wreath.

"Good morning to you, Ebbé. I regret you had a sleepless night," said a low-pitched voice. "As to your question, I can help you if you would like."

Ebbé looked up into the branches of the large tree he had slept under. The trunk was thick. Ribbons of bark coiled around it like a boa stretching itself down to the ground, where it twisted and turned a distance before slipping, headfirst, into the ground. The branches were thicker than Ebbé's body and extended out from the tree, forming a protective roof over the forest. It stood alone, allowing no other tree, not even as much as a root, to cross into its magical circle.

The sunlight filtered down through the leaves, where pinpoints of sun flakes danced on the ground. At times, if one was lucky, a wood faerie could be seen waltzing among the trees. Some would say they were simply sun flakes, but the lucky ones—the ones with imagination knew better.

The wood faeries were drawn into the protective sheath that surrounded the giant tree. They knew instinctively they would be safe to dance within it. Butterflies would flutter into the defused light within the ring, the boldest of them asking one of the faeries to join them in a dance. The wood faerie would tip her head and smile, and the twirling of wings would begin.

The music they waltzed to was supplied by a chorus of crickets, birds, and frogs, their notes spinning around the dancing couples. The faster the tempo, the more faerie dust clouded the air. When there were several couples dancing and when the music's pace was quick, anyone sitting outside the tree's sheath could see a whirlwind of sparkling dust swirling around the trunk. Long after the dancing had stopped, the sparkling dust hung in the air until it tired of waiting for the music to start again and slowly sparkled its way to the ground.

Ebbé felt the strength of the tree and yielded to its wisdom. He felt protected in its presence. "I'm looking toward my future and for answers, if you could, to any questions that may help me understand it," Ebbé, he said, his voice dwindling as he looked up into the expansive canopy.

"Sometimes, Ebbé, we may choose our future, but other times our future chooses us. Life has many different paths, and each one takes us in different directions and down different paths. There is no right or wrong path, since each leads us to new discoveries. Life, after all, is nothing more than the gathering of knowledge. Do you understand this concept, Ebbé?"

Ebbé bowed his head as he brushed the grass around with his foot while giving thought to what the tree had said. Ebbé knew he had a great deal to learn before his journey turned him around and faced him back toward his home and family.

"Ebbé, have I lost you, or are you just deep in thought? You must learn to read yourself from the inside out; 'tis simple when one becomes accomplished in the technique to do so. Ebbé, I fear at times you are far too serious for your own good. You squeeze out the pathway that lets your instincts flow. "Open your heart and mind, and you will be awed by the world that reveals itself to you." The tree gave a deep-throated chuckle. "Yes, I do sound just like your father."

Ebbé was caught sideways by the remark; he had recognized his father's words echoing in those of the guide, who was disguised as this majestic tree.

Ebbé picked up his knapsack, stepped back a few paces, and bowed to the tree. He turned and left the warm, magical place where he had spent the night. He had found a piece of the puzzle.

The late spring morning still carried a nip of cold air, but the sun's heat was beginning to warm Ebbé up. He crossed a meadow full of lavender. He stopped, took a deep breath, and smiled. He looked up and saw some butterflies dancing in the breeze, and he paused to watch them.

Ebbé came to a stream, took off his shoes and socks, and rolled up his pant legs. He then pulled his small sled through the water. When he got to the other side, he dropped the rope and went back to stand in the stream. It was shallow, and the water was warm and tickled his ankles as it slipped by. Ebbé decided it was a good place to spend the night. And so he did.

That night, lying by his small, warm fire, Ebbé thought of his home and the long summer days when he would play down by the river that ran past his village. With his eyes closed, he could see and smell the hickory-scented fire in the village center. Ebbé licked his lips as he imagined tasting the meat roasting on the spit. That made him hungry, so he decided to do some fishing the next day. Tomorrow night he would have his own feast. He would catch a big trout and cook it over a fire. He went to sleep with the aroma on his mind.

In the morning, Ebbé packed up the sled and went in search of a good fishing hole.

He morning warmed in the smiling heat of the sun. He sat down under a small tree and smiled. *Such a nice day,* he thought. He took some nuts and berries out of his knapsack and replaced them with his folded blanket. He liked things neat and always in their place. This trait had been handed down to him from his mother's side.

Ebbé put the serviette down on the green grass and placed his breakfast on it. He poured some water from the canteen into his tin cup and set it down by the serviette. Keeping familiar patterns helped him stave off the loneliness he felt at times. When he had finished the meal, he placed everything neatly back in its appointed place. Feeling sleepy, Ebbé decided a nap was a better option than walking nowhere, so he put his head down on his knapsack and closed his eyes.

It wasn't but a wink of a second when Ebbé heard a plop. He looked over to a tree not far from him and saw that a baby bird had fallen out of its nest. "Are you okay over there?" Ebbé called out. He stood up and walked over to see if the tiny bird was all right. Approaching the bird, he asked, "Do you think anything is broken?"

The little bird was twisting his head around so he could see his backside. "Yes, I think so," he said, lifting his wings so Ebbé could look him over and asked. "Do you see any feathers sticking out anywhere?"

Ebbé made a slow circle around the little bird and saw some feathers sticking out at an odd angle. "I think you have a broken wing, little guy. Does it hurt?" He looked at the baby bird, hoping he wasn't in too much pain. He knelt down and asked, "Why didn't you just fly down? It would have been easier."

The little bird stood there looking up at Ebbé. Rolling his eyes, he answered, "Ya think?" He flapped his good wing and fluffed the feathers until he felt they were all back in their rightful place. Then he looked at his broken wing, wondering what he was going to do now. "For your

Freefall

information, I don't fly. Never learned. I never wanted to. The idea of wings covered with feathers being all that's keeping me up, well, just seems sort of unnatural to me.".

"My siblings left the nest a few days ago, and my parents told me to fly or fall, but either way it was time to leave the nest. I was getting hungry, so I decided to go for it. Thinking the problem was all in my head, I got up on top of the nest, closed my eyes, and jumped. Before I could get my wings flapping, the trip down was over. Uff da, what a rush!" He shook his head, remembering the short trip.

Ebbé was beginning to think something funny had happened to the little bird's thinking. "Do you have a name?" he asked.

The baby bird looked up at Ebbé. "No, I don't. We're named after our first flight." He thought a moment. "Do you think this trip will count? It was short, but I may have gotten a flap off before landing. Push come to shove, it was a short flight. What do 'ya think?"

"It was close enough, little guy. Let me think a minute about a name for you." Ebbé closed his eyes, rubbed his chin, and pondered. "Hmm, you didn't actually fly down; you just kind of fell down."

The little bird was growing impatient. After all, it couldn't be that hard to pick a name.

"I've got it! I have the perfect name for you. How about Freefall? That's how you got down. It fits."

"Freefall," the little bird said, rolling the name off his tongue. "I like it a lot! It really fits me."

"Yes, it does. Freefall. It couldn't fit better. By the way, my name is Ebbé. Tell me, what are you going to do now that you are grounded with a broken wing?"

Shaking his head, Freefall looked at Ebbé and said, "I have no idea."

"Well, it seems you and I are on our own. You're welcome to come with me on my journey. We'll figure out how to fix your wing and get you airborne." Ebbé looked at Freefall and smiled. "Actually it would be nice to have company. What do you say?"

"I won't be able to travel as fast as you, Ebbé."

"Well, I'll just give you a ride then." Ebbé reached down and gently picked up Freefall and carried him over to his sled. He secured his knapsack onto the sled and placed Freefall on top. "Does your wing hurt?"

"It does hurt some. Well, a lot really," Freefall answered as he swiped at a tear rolling down his face. Ebbé patted Freefall on his soft, fluffy head and said, "It's going to be all right, little guy. You'll see. Now, hold on." Freefall smiled up at Ebbé and was happy, for now he had a name and a friend.

◖◉◗

The trees thinned out, allowing more of the sun's heat to find its way to the forest floor. Rainbow-colored flowers dotted the ground, appearing as if confetti had been tossed up into the air in celebration and then landed everywhere. The day's warmth invited all the forest creatures to venture outside.

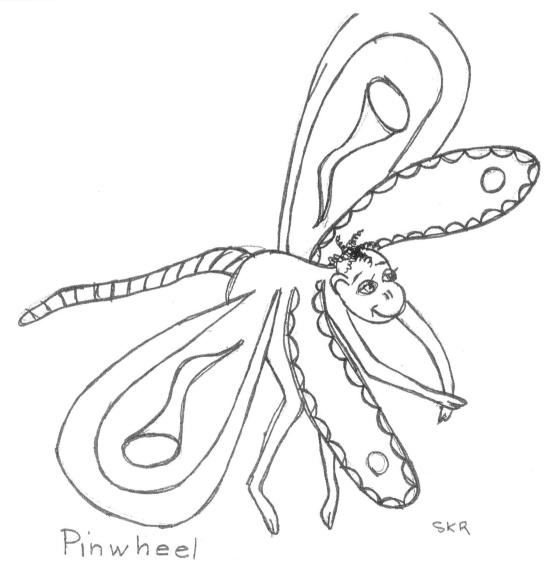

Pinwheel

SKR

Two dragonflies fluttered circles around Ebbé and Freefall. "Hi, we're Hoverine and Pinwheel. Where are you headed to?" they asked in unison, for that is what dragonflies do.

"We're looking for Ebbé's future," Freefall answered. Ebbé placed Freefall on the ground so he could stretch his wing and legs. He sat down beside his sled and looked up at the two dragonflies, cupping his hands over his eyes to keep the glare of the sunlight away. He reached for his canteen and took a long drink of water and then poured some in the lid for Freefall. The dragonflies fluttered down to a rock and settled in. "Have you been in these lands for long?"

"Just since early spring," answered Ebbé.

"Ebbé found me, and he's going to teach me to fly after my broken wing heals!" Freefall exclaimed.

"Are you okay? Does it hurt?" Hoverine and Pinwheel asked.

"It does, but not so much as it did," Freefall answered.

"After it heals, we can help you learn to fly, the dragonflies said. We know all about flying. We'll have you airborne in no time.".

"That would be great, you two!" Ebbé exclaimed. "It may take a while for his wing to heal, but by summer's end, Freefall should have his flying down pat."

For the next few days, Ebbé and the dragonflies kept their eyes on Freefall. They sat and watched for his little wing to heal. "It still looks funny. Kinda sticks out at an odd angle, don't ya think?" Pinwheel said. Hoverine agreed that it did.

They spent the next few weeks watching Freefall's wing and waiting for it to look like his good wing. "I'm afraid, Freefall, your wing has healed at an odd angle," Ebbé said while Freefall turned around with both of his wings out so Ebbé could compare them. "Nope, they're different looking, for sure."

Ebbé and the two dragonflies had Freefall exercise his wings to make them stronger.

"Flap them faster," Ebbé said to Freefall.

"But what if I start to lift off, Ebbé?"

"Then flap even faster."

The dragonflies showed him how to place his wings so the air could flow over them for lift, but Freefall couldn't get any lift off the broken one. "Now what am I gonna do?" a frustrated little Freefall asked. "Every time I start to get liftoff, my broken wing stops me. Now what?!"

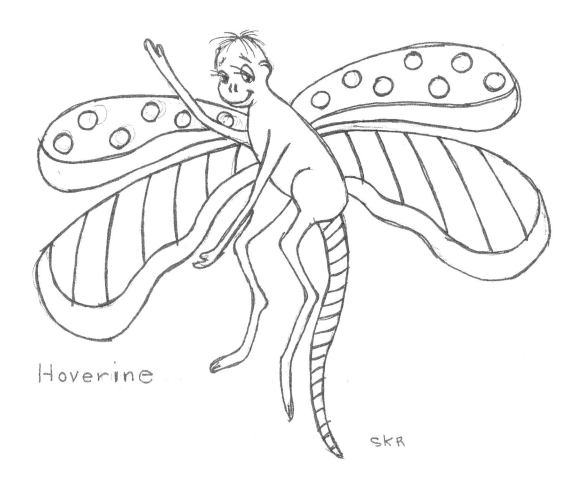

Hoverine

SKR

Hoverine and Pinwheel watched Freefall as he struggled again to get airborne. "Seems to me," Pinwheel said, "your broken wing isn't getting any lift. Try lifting the wing up as high as you can as you start to take off."

Freefall started his run with his broken wing held as high as he could. And he got airborne, if only for a few moments.

"Well, at least he got off the ground this time, Pinwheel," Hoverine said.

"Yep, I think the little guy will get airborne soon now," answered Pinwheel.

Ebbé watched Freefall and listened to the two dragonflies, and he hoped Freefall would be able to fly someday soon.

◀◉ ◉▶

Soon Freefall was leaving the ground for short hops. After a few days of lessons, the two dragonflies decided it was time to go. They wanted to flutter about the area and see what they could see.

"Good journey to you, Ebbé," they said. "Freefall, we hope to see you sky bound one day. Remember to keep that wing held high on liftoff. And remember if you want something, you have to work at it. You'll get there." the dragonflies said in unison.

"You two take care of yourselves," Ebbé said. "And thanks for working with Freefall. I'll remember what you showed us, and I'll make sure he does his workouts every day so he gets stronger. I know he'll be sky bound one day soon."

"Thank you for helping me," Freefall added with a big smile. "I'm going to remember everything you showed me and work on my lessons every day."

The two dragonflies were off to their next adventure.

In that land, everyone seemed to drift in and out of each others lives, picking up friendships that were left around the corner. They always came back with new tales to tell and knowledge to share. This was the way of the realm, all of the creatures swept up by a sudden wind and then set back down to wait for the wind to take them on their next journey.

Ebbé waved to the dragonflies until they were out of sight. He bent down, and as he picked up the sled rope, Freefall jumped onto the sled. "Good for you," Ebbé said. "See, it won't be too long before you'll be flying. But your sky will be larger than Hoverine and Pinwheel will ever know. Just wait, you'll see."

Freefall looked up into the beautiful blue of the day, knowing it was his heritage. "Someday I'm going to touch the clouds," he whispered. "I'm going to work as hard as I can."

❦

Ebbé and Freefall traveled from flower-covered meadow to green forest, back to another flower-covered meadow. One day they were lying down in a meadow covered with yellow wildflowers and watch the snow-white clouds change shapes as they floated by.

"Do you miss your family, Freefall?" Ebbé asked. He was lying on his back with a sweet-tasting blade of grass in his mouth. Freefall lay next to him with his wings stretched out to air his feathers.

"Birds, Ebbé, are never a family like trolls. We're given life and taught the lessons we'll need. When the time comes, we're sent off to venture out into the world. Sometimes, if we stay in the area, we may see family about. I had one sibling who never made fun of me because I was afraid to fly. He tried to help me, but he had his own adventures to discover." He paused, wiggling his talons about. "What's it like to have a family?"

Ebbé worked the blade of grass around in his mouth. "Families sometimes have their differences, but we're always there for each other. It's all about love and caring, Freefall, and helping each other grow in spirit."

"Is that why you're on your journey, so you can grow in spirit? Are you growing good, Ebbé?"

Ebbé gave a chuckle and looked over at Freefall. Such different worlds and ways had come from. One was loved and nurtured through their lifetime, and one was set out on a path alone. That seemed sad to Ebbé. "Someday you'll be a magnificent falcon," he said, "that soars high in the heavens with no boundaries and nothing to hold you to a straight line like in my world. So, I guess we're both lucky in our different ways."

For a long time the two friends lay among the flowers, staring up at the blue sky, each lost in their own thoughts.

"The day is stepping to the warm side," Ebbé said. "Let's find a tree and have something to eat. How does that sound to you?"

"Like a good idea, Ebbé."

They found a nice shade tree, and Ebbé laid out the serviette and placed their noon dinner on it. After finishing their usual meal of nuts and berries, they washed in a small pond and then decided to take a nap. Ebbé placed his head on his rolled-up cape and closed his eyes. He was just about to drift off when he heard something off in the bushes. "Hello, is anybody there? Did you hear anything, Freefall?" asked Ebbé in a quiet voice.

"I did," Freefall, answered, tucking himself a little deeper into the grass. They heard more rustling and sat up to take a closer listen. Just then, another sound came from the bushes. Deciding to peek, they got up and tiptoed over to the bush very slowly. "Stay behind me," whispered Ebbé.

They tried their best to be as quiet as possible. Holding his breath, Ebbé bent over and very carefully parted the bush just enough to peek. There, hiding in the bush, curled up in a ball with his eyes closed, was a baby lemming. Keeping his eyes shut as tightly as he could, he kept repeating aloud, "There's no one there. There's no one there."

Looking down at the scared baby lemming, Ebbé said very softly, so as not to frighten him, "We're here, Freefall and me, Ebbé. We won't hurt you."

"If I open my eyes up, just a little, you won't eat me?"

NIBBLETS

Ebbé smiled and answered, "No, of course not, little guy."

"Well then, I'll open my left eye to see what an Ebbé looks like, and then I'll close my Ebbé eye and open my right eye to see what a Freefall looks like. Is that okay?"

"If you open both your eyes together, you'll see us at the same time."Ebbé said.

"Well, now I'm confused! If I open my eyes up at the same time, how am I gonna know the difference between an Ebbé and a Freefall, 'cause I won't know which eye is looking at who!"

Ebbé and Freefall looked at each other, trying not to giggle. "Just open both your eyes together, and we'll introduce ourselves to you," Ebbé answered.

"Okay, but only if you count to three. Let me take a deep breath first."

So the tiny lemming took a deep breath and said, "I'm ready now."

With that, Ebbé and Freefall counted "One... two... three."

The baby lemming opened his left eye a bit and then his right eye a little, and peeked out and saw a bird not much bigger than he and a troll not much bigger than the bird. "Hello," he said, looking out from his hiding place.

"Hello, I'm Ebbé," Ebbé said, putting his hand to his chest as he introduced himself. He nudged Freefall forward so the lemming could see him and added, "This is Freefall."

"My name is Nibblets, and I think it's nice to meet you."

"Well, it's our pleasure to meet you, Nibblets. Where is your family?"

"I don't know where anybody is anymore," he answered, putting his head down.

"What happened?" asked Freefall.

"I seem to have lost them. We were being chased. I couldn't keep up with them, 'cause when I try to run fast, my bottom backside starts a'swishin' and rolls me over. Then I have to kick my legs really fast to get my bottom backside down so I can run again." After taking a long deep breath, Nibblets continued, "I was running behind my family, trying my best to keep up, when I did a rollover and got covered in leaves. By the time I was back to being right side up, everybody was gone! I've been hiding here in the bushes with my eyes shut tight so nobody would see me, but I don't know for how long, 'cause I'm too little to tell time." Nibblets took a deep breath and tried his best not to cry.

"It's going to be just fine, Nibblets," Ebbé said. "We'll take care of you, and we'll be your family now. How does that sound?" He hoped that would make little Nibblets feel better.

"You won't go so fast that I'll do another rollover?"

"No, you can ride on my sled alongside of Freefall. There is room enough for both of you. How does that sound to you?"

"It sounds good. Just let me take a deep breath, and I'll be ready."

Nibblets came out of the bushes, and the three new friends walked back over to the tree. Ebbé bent down and picked little Nibblets up, noted how soft he was, and placed him on the sled. Freefall hopped up, sat beside Nibblets, and smiled, hoping it would make the little guy feel safer. "Are we ready?" Ebbé asked.

"Yes," Freefall and Nibblets answered. And so the threesome set off on the journey to find their futures.

Ebbé had started his journey alone, and he now found himself with two younglings to take care of. He remembered the words of the guide disguised as a tree: "Sometimes we may choose our future, and sometimes our future chooses us." He liked what his future had chosen for him. It would be fun to nurture these babes and watch them grow. He would make sure to give them the best he could, his two little friends.

☙❧

One afternoon they were lying out in a sweet-smelling meadow, resting in the sun's warmth after having a very busy morning of doing nothing.

"What is a future, Ebbé?" Nibblets asked.

"Well, let me think," Ebbé answered, lying with the usual blade of grass in his mouth. "You can't see it from here. I'm not sure as to when we'll see it, because I don't know how far away a future is."

"If you don't know what a future is, or where it is, Ebbé, how are we going to know it when we find it?" asked Freefall.

"We'll just have to see as we go. And while we're on our way, we'll teach you how to fly, Freefall. We need to get started on your lessons again. After our noon dinner, we'll make a plan, okay?"

Looking over at Ebbé, Nibblets said, "You're so smart, Ebbé. I feel so safe with you, and it's going to be so much fun to watch Freefall fly."

"We'll teach you how to run with your back feet out so you don't do rollovers anymore," Freefall told Nibblets.

"When I walk, I could go faster so you don't have to walk so slowly," Nibblets said. "My bottom gets so sore swishing so much, I'm afraid it might fall completely off!" Nibblets said.

Freefall laughed. "Uff da! Bottoms don't fall off."

"Gosh, I hope not, 'cause I'd only have half of me to walk with!"

"You worry too much, Nibblets," Ebbé said. "When you walk, I'll go slow and make sure you never get lost again."

Tomorrow came, and it was time for Freefall's first flying lesson. They were standing in the middle of a small honey-scented meadow. Ebbé licked his finger and held it up to test which way the wind was blowing. "It's coming from the west, so that's the direction you'll want to take off into."

Freefall was flapping his wings, warming them up. "I've got a head start 'cause the dragonflies showed me how to flap my wings. I just need to know what to do after I take off. How do I stay up in the air, Ebbé? And how do I get back down?" Freefall shook his head and added "Uff da! There's sure a lot to know about flying."

"You'll do just fine, Freefall," Ebbé said. "We'll do just one lesson at a time. First, we'll find a low tree branch for you to hop up to. This will help you with your liftoff and landing skills. And while Freefall is doing his lessons, Nibblets, you can practice running with your back legs out so you don't roll over. Are we ready?"

Out in the meadow, among the wildflowers, could be seen a little bird doing hop-ups onto tree limbs; a baby lemming running as fast as he could in circles with his back legs out as far as he could get them; and a small troll clapping his hands and yelling out encouragements to them: "That's it, Nibblets, keep your back legs out just the way you have them. Great landing, Freefall. Next time, find something higher to land on."

That afternoon they were rewarded with a nice long nap for a morning well spent. The next few days they worked on their lessons and talked about their futures.

One afternoon, during their usual naptime, Nibblets asked, "Does now count as the future, or is the future something that comes after today? I'm confused again, Ebbé."

"As far as my thinking goes, today is now; and it's the now that we live in on our way to the future. Does this make any sense?" Ebbé asked.

"I think so, but how do I know the difference between the now and the future? If one follows the other, when does it go from one to the other?"

Ebbé gave it some thought and answered, "You have a past, like yesterday, and then you have now. Each moment we live becomes the past."

"You are so confusing me, Ebbé!" said Freefall. "I don't know if I'm coming or going, and when was it I started going and not coming?"

Rolling over on the ground, Nibblets said, "Oh, Ebbé, you're so smart, and I don't understand any of it. I'm going to take a deep breath and then take a nap, 'cause my future is getting a headache."

"Try thinking of it as a leaf floating downstream, always on the move, going from moment to moment," Ebbé said, talking to no one, since he was the only one awake. "I think my future needs a nap too."

The spring days warmed to the smile of summer, and their time was spent between lessons and simply enjoying the new surprises each day brought. One afternoon Ebbé was meadow sitting with a blade of grass in his mouth, watching Freefall fly, when he heard two familiar voices say in unison. "Hi there, Ebbé."

He looked up to see Hoverine and Pinwheel fluttering about.

"Hey, guys, nice to see you," Ebbé answered.

"Is that our Freefall over there, doing touch-and-goes?"

Ebbé was sitting with his knees up and his arms resting on them. He looked up at Freefall with pride. "Sure is. He flies higher each day."

"Who's that over there, running in circles?"

"That would be Nibblets. We found him hiding under a bush not too long after you left. He's been running around for a while now, so it's just about time for his nap. He poops himself out quickly."

Freefall was about to come in for a landing when he spotted the two dragonflies. He gave a big smile, flew back up, did a circle, and landed by them. "What do you think? Bet you never thought you'd see me doing that. I love flying. I love it!"

"You've got good form there," Pinwheel said. "You know, Freefall, I think the odd angle might help you do loop-de-loops dragonfly style. You'll be the only bird I know who will be able to do that."

"Ya think, Pinwheel? Really?" Freefall had a big grin.

"Hey, he's sure changed," Hoverine said. "Went and got himself some confidence."

"He's got the makings of a darn good bird," answered Pinwheel.

"Here comes Nibblets," Ebbé said.

Nibblets had finally pooped out and was coming over to sit down beside Ebbé, who introduced him to the dragonflies. They watched as Hoverine and Pinwheel showed Freefall the fine art of loop-de-loops dragonfly style. Ebbé smiled and thought it was true: his little friend had gone and gotten himself grown up. It made him happy to know he had been part of it.

That night, the small gathering of friends was a bit bigger at supper. They talked about all the new discoveries they had made. They shared news of different places and the comings and goings of the realm. The wind had picked the dragonflies up and again placed them by Ebbé, just as he knew it would.

"Tell Hoverine and Pinwheel what a future is, Ebbé," Nibblets said.

"Okay. Well, to put it as simply as I can." Ebbé thought about it for a moment and then said, "A future is a brightly wrapped present just waiting for us to open."

Freefall smiled and said, "I like that, Ebbé. It doesn't confuse me at all."

"I'm happy you understand about a future now. It's not so confusing after all, is it?" Ebbé answered.

"We're so lucky to have you as our friend. I like you lots, Ebbé" Nibblets said, looking up at Ebbé.

"We make a good family, don't we." Freefall said, smiling, realizing that he really was part of a family.

Ebbé made a small fire for light and warmth. It cast a red glow around the small group of friends. He liked the idea that he had brought them into his colored sheath filled with love. He looked around at each one and felt great pride and true blessing.

"Tell us, Ebbé, what kind of future are you looking for?" Freefall asked.

Ebbé stared into the crackling flames and thought it out before giving his answer. "Well, I'd like to be what my father sees when he looks at me. He's tried to teach me to believe in myself, but it's me that has to learn this lesson. "In our realm of the trolls, we go about our business and live as we have since the beginning. But outside our realm, we're looked upon with dislike. The human realm doesn't really know us. They only know what has been passed down in their folklore. They don't even know we really exist.

"I cannot change a belief system that has been in place for so long. I wish I could. We all are different, but it's our differences that we should cherish in each other. We have so much to learn from one another." Ebbé stopped and stared into the fire, and in a quiet voice said, "Every time I look into a pond and see my reflection, I see me. I see my long old nose, and my hair sticks out every which way."

He looked down at his feet then held out his hands and looked at them. "Look at my hands and feet. They're so big, they look funny. I wish I didn't look like me. I wish I was a handsome troll."

All his friends were quiet, trying to think of something they could say to cheer him up. They had never seen this side of Ebbé. They didn't know how to react to what he said, so they just put their heads down and pondered it.

It was a black, moonless night. A chilly breeze walked through where they sat. All the other forest creatures had long since gone to bed, leaving the night to them.

"Look at that light over there, Ebbé," whispered Nibblets. "What do you think it can be?"

"I don't know, but it seems to be heading this way," Ebbé whispered back.

"I hope it's nothing we have to run from, 'cause I'm not sure that I've got my running down pat; I don't know how I'd do."

Ebbé put his arm around Nibblets, who snuggled in closer to him, feeling safe and protected. They all moved in close to each other, watching the light in the sky becoming brighter as it drew nearer to their small gathering.

Just when they were deciding what to do, a beautiful forest faerie appeared from out of the center of the glowing light. She was cousin to the wood faerie, taller and more slender in build. Her copper hair lay in soft curls, like a shawl around her shoulders. A wreath of tiny shimmering butterflies fluttered around her head.

Her dress, the palest shade of ivory, softly danced about her body, giving her the appearance of perpetual movement. She gave off a distinct scent of vanilla, as all faeries do. Her opalescent wings made a soft windy sound as her tiny pointed toes gently touched the ground.

"Hello. A pleasant evening to you," she said in her lyrical voice. She looked at Ebbé. "I've been listening, Ebbé, and I've come to explain some things to you."

She reached out her hands to him, and he slowly stood up, wondering what this beautiful forest faerie would want with the likes of him. He put his hands into hers.

"Ebbé, my dear little troll," she said. "I've been watching you for a long time. I've seen the tenderness you give to each of your friends. You have such patience, and you have helped each of them grow in ways they never imagined they could. May I sit down beside you until morning?"

So the small gathering of friends snuggled up and slept peacefully, bathed in the vanilla scent that surrounded them.

(( ))

Dawn woke up and mixed pink and blue together on her palate, then splashed it across the sky. The group of friends slowly began to wake up. They stretched out arms and wings, but were not yet ready to shake off the mystical vanilla warmth that had cocooned them through the night.

One by one, they gathered their thoughts, each wondering what this newly born day would bring. When everyone was awake, the forest faerie announced that it was time for her to leave. She bent over, took Ebbé's face in her hands, and kissed his forehead.

"Will this make me a handsome troll?" he asked, hoping it would. She smiled and answered, "No, my dear Ebbé, it will not. I want you to close your eyes and put your face up to the morning sun, and tell me what you feel."

With her hands on his shoulder, he did as she asked.

"I feel a warm feeling all over me. I feel the sunshine."

"How does it make you feel?"

"It makes me happy," Ebbé answered with a big smile. He opened his eyes and looked at her.

"Ebbé, when we look at you, this is what we feel. What we see is your heart, as pure and warm as the sun's light. When you look into the water and see your reflection, you see only the outside of you. When we look at you, we see your loving inside. Never forget this, for it is the most important discovery you will make on the journey toward your future."

"What do you think it might be?"

"The future will be what you want it to be; as you said, it is simply a brightly wrapped present just waiting for us to open." She paused. "I think your future will be giving the gift of your heart, the gift of love. Look around you, Ebbé. You've made a wonderful start already." She paused. "My sisters and I will always be near you." Then she looked at the small group of friends and said, "All of you."

"How will we know you are near, pretty faerie?" asked Nibblets.

"By my vanilla scent in the air, little one. That's how you know when a faerie is near." She looked at each friend. "We are here to watch over you."

"We love our Ebbé lots and lots," Nibblets said, smiling up at the beautiful forest faerie.

"I know you do, little one," she answered, patting Nibblets's head.

The group gathered into a circle with the faerie as she gave a blessing for this wondrous day and wished each one a safe journey and a bright future. Then, in the wink of their eyes, she was gone. All that remained where she had been were sprinkles of golden dust that shimmered as they tiptoed slowly to the ground, leaving only the scent of vanilla behind.

A new day had begun, bringing new discoveries and life lessons to learn. It was hard to break the spell she had cast on them, but it was time to continue on to their futures.

"Do you think we'll ever see her again, Ebbé?" Freefall asked.

"I can't answer that. I hope so. I hope we do," Ebbé answered, still lost in the faerie glow.

"May Pinwheel and I join you on your journey, Ebbé? We're curious to see just what a future looks like."

"Of course. We'd love to have your company," answered Ebbé.

"Hey, we can do some flying together." Freefall was excited about the idea of learning more about the art of loop-de-loops dragonfly style.

As the morning passed into noon, the small group of friends could be seen making their way through another meadow: a small troll that didn't think of himself as ugly; a little bird flying in circles, playing chase with two dragonflies; and a baby lemming running around, keeping his back legs out so as not to do a rollover. And throughout the day they paused, trying to catch the scent of vanilla in the air.

The long, hot summer days were slowly winding down. All the creatures of the forest were beginning to store supplies for the cold winter months that lay ahead. Nibblets was as big as he was going to get, which was still little. He practiced his running lessons daily.

Ebbé said, "I think you'll do just fine in a pinch, Nibblets, if you ever need to make a quick getaway. You have great form in your running now."

"Thanks, Ebbé. I'm glad it was you and Freefall who found me. I love you lots." And off he ran to make a few more circles in the meadow.

Freefall had his flying down pat. He had feathered out into a grand-looking falcon. Ebbé loved nothing better than to watch him soar in the sky—the way he climbed straight up and then slowly glided down in a spiral on the hidden staircase in the sky, as Freefall called the thermals.

Pinwheel and Hoverine couldn't keep up with him anymore. "Uff da, Pinwheel, look at him go straight up!" Hoverine said. His flying amazed them. And Ebbé was proud to see how his two friends had grown.

Freefall spread his wings and landed by Ebbé, who was sitting in the meadow, watching him.

"Boy, Ebbé, I can't believe I was so afraid to fly. Wasn't that silly of me?"

"No, not really. You were just a baby bird when I met you, but I knew you would fly like this someday. You just had to grow up."

After running his morning circles in the meadow, Nibblets came over and plopped down beside them. He took in a deep breath of the sweet morning air said, "I sure wish Freefall could take me for a ride, Ebbé. Wouldn't that be fun?"

"Yes, it would be, little buddy."

Pinwheel and Hoverine had been playing chase and watching Freefall do some grand loop-de-loops. "It would be fun to fly as high as he goes," the dragonflies said. "No bird could ever catch him now. Look at him go!"

Ebbé waved at Freefall as he did one more loop and landed beside the group.

"Well, now that we're all here," Ebbé said, "we should make a plan for winter; it's not too far away. We need to find a home for the winter and start gathering food. We'll have to work together. The days are still warm, but it won't be long before the land will be covered with winter's snow."

"Pinwheel and I will do some scouting for berry patches and then fly back and let you know where they are," Hoverine said.

"Great idea. That will save us a lot of footwork," Ebbé answered.

"I can go look for a burrow for us to winter in!" exclaimed Nibblets.

"And I can start gathering some moss and twigs to line it so we'll stay warm," chimed in Freefall.

"Well, looks like we'll be just fine with everybody working together. I think we'll have a nice, cozy winter." Ebbé smiled, pleased with the way they were working as a team. And off they went, all in different directions, to spend the afternoon doing their tasks.

❀

Pinwheel and Hoverine found some ripe berry patches not too far away. "Boy, this will make Ebbé happy," Pinwheel said. "Look at all these juicy berries just waiting to be picked. Let's fly back and tell Ebbé so everyone can start picking them." So off they flew, back to where they'd started.

In the meantime, Ebbé was busy weaving grasses together for knapsacks they would need to put berries in. He loved sitting there in the sunshine while doing his tasks. Feeling the warmth of the sun on his face always reminded him of the forest faerie and what she had said to him about his heart and his future. He tried to catch the scent of vanilla in the air. He hoped she was watching from somewhere above and was proud of him. He was doing the best he could, and it was an easy task for him. "I think it will be a good winter for us," he said aloud to himself.

"Ebbé! Ebbé!" It was Nibblets running as fast as he could through the meadow. "Ebbé, I found us our home. Oh, it's so nice, and we have neighbors too, Ebbé. Come see." He ran up to Ebbé and flopped down beside him, out of breath. "I ran all the way as fast as I could. Oh, I'm so pooped."

"Good job," Ebbé said, smiling. "Just lie here a minute and catch your breath. Then you can tell me all about it."

Nibblets rolled over onto his back and closed his eyes and took some deep breaths. "I'm feeling better now, Ebbé. I just ran so fast without stopping. I can't wait for you to see our new home and meet our neighbors."

"When you're feeling rested, you can tell me all about it, Nibblets," Ebbé answered, excited to hear all about this new home little Nibblets had found for them.

Nibblets took another breath, counted to three, and began. "Our winter home is under a big old tree, not too far from here. It's just inside the woods, right over there." He pointed over to the edge of the meadow. "See, Ebbé? Right over there. And Nibblets pointed over to the edge of the meadow. "There's Mrs. Latchshaw. She's a rabbit and has four younglings, Miley, Nutmeg, Marionberry, and Cornflower. And Freefall will be happy, 'cause a bird lives in the top of our tree. He's a pretty white owl and flies almost as good our Freefall does."

"Well now, sounds like you found the perfect home for us," Ebbé said. "Let's go see it, and you can introduce me to our new friends." Off they went, at a slower pace for Nibblets, to see their new winter home.

Nibblets had indeed found them the perfect home. The burrow was deep and large enough, so there would be plenty of room for all of them. The tree that the burrow was under was a splendid spruce, and Ebbé felt sure they would be safe under its protection.

Raindrip

"Hello, Ebbé," said a voice from up in the tree. Ebbé looked up to see a beautiful white owl.

The owl flew down from the branch and landed next to Ebbé and Nibblets. "Welcome to my forest," he said. "I'm Raindrip. I saw the dragonflies zooming through here. They certainly are busy creatures with their minds set on berry finding. There are plenty of berry patches for all, so please help yourselves. The fruit stays long, so there is a good supply into winter.

"This has been my home for more winters than I can remember. This is Mrs. Latchshaw's fourth winter here, different younglings though. I must say, this year's batch seems to be smarter than her last." Raindrip shook his head, remembering. "We also have a miniature reindeer named Rooka. He does patrols for us. So between us, we keep our patch of this forest protected and safe."

"I'm sure Freefall would like to help you out there," Ebbé said. "If you don't mind, that is."

"No problem, the more eyes the better. Snow can get deep here in the winter, and there's always someone who goes missing. Never fails. But we always find them. They come out cold, but smarter."

"How did you get your name?" Nibblets asked, looking up at Raindrip.

"Well, little one," Raindrip answered, "when I was just a little skittle, I was the one unlucky enough to have the place in the nest where the rain dripped down, right on top of my head. Drip after drip after drip. And that is the story behind my name."

"Good morning, there," said a voice from behind Ebbé.

"Oh, I betcha anything you're Nibblets's Ebbé. My, my! This little guy talks a mile a minute. Such a sweet little thing," she said without taking a breath as she patted Nibbler's head. "I already think of him as one of my own. I'm Mrs. Latchshaw, by the way, and pleased to meet you."

She took a breath and continued, "Oh wonders! I think it's going to be a happy winter having you folks here. It's always nice to have a group around for the winter. I always say, the more, the merrier. Days can get long if you don't have anyone to visit with, and your little Nibblets will have fun times with my four younglings. It keeps them busy. Oh, my, I forgot to tell you; that's our burrow right under that tree over there." She pointed. "Just a hop and a skip away."

Ebbé, feeling out of breath just listening to her, could only nod in agreement.

Ebbé looked at the two small rabbits walking toward them, carrying knapsacks, with the two dragonflies fluttering around them. "Nibblets, can you come pick berries with us, the rabbits asked?"

"Well, Nibblets, these must be your new friends," Ebbé said.

"They are, Ebbé. They're Miley and Nutmeg. Oh, I'm gonna have a fun winter here. May I go pick berries with them?"

"Of course you may," Ebbé answered, handing Nibblets a knapsack. "I made this for you to take berry picking. You might as well gather some for us too."

"Oh my, thank you, Ebbé. I'll get us the biggest and juiciest ones I can pick."

"We'll help him reach the good ones at the top, Mr. Ebbé," said Nutmeg. "Pinwheel and Hoverine can help also."

Mrs Latchshaw

Miley smiled at little Nibblets and said, "And we'll all help Nibblets carry his knapsack back, seeing how he's too small to manage it himself."

"I'm pretty big for me, you guys," Nibblets answered, standing as tall as he could.

"We know you are, Nibblets," Nutmeg said. "But just in case it gets too heavy for you, we'll help."

The five set off, with Nibblets dragging his sack behind him; it was already bigger than he was, and it wasn't even full of berries.

"Bye. Be careful, and take care of Nibblets," Mrs. Latchshaw yelled behind them. "And mind you, don't get yourselves into any trouble." Mrs. Latchshaw yelled behind them. But they didn't hear her; they were already too busy having fun.

They came to the berry patch and saw it was ripe with berries just waiting for them to go about the business of berry picking. "Now the idea is to pick more than we eat," said Miley.

"Yeah, Miley," answered Nutmeg. "You said that last time we went berry picking, and you went home sick!"

"You ate just as many as I did, Nutmeg. You were just lucky 'cause you didn't get sick, so I was the one who got in trouble with mama."

"Got ya that time!"

"Well, this time we'd better make sure we pick more than we eat; winter is just about here."

"Sometimes Rooka comes along, and we climb up on his back so we can pick the very top berries," Miley said.

"Yeah, that's fun!" exclaimed Nutmeg. "Best part is sliding back down off his back. If he were here, he'd let you climb up too."

Miley

Miley, Nutmeg and Nibblets) place pictures of the 3 down to drag-onflies pondered the idea of going for help) "Oh gosh, that would be so much fun," Nibblets said, trying to picture himself trying to jump up on Rooka's back. "But I don't know if I could get up, 'cause I'm too little to hop up like you guys do."

"That's okay. We'd give you a leg up," said Nutmeg.

"Hey, I have an idea," Miley said. "Pinwheel and Hoverine, why don't you fly up to the top of the berry bush and pick some of those juicy berries at the top. You can drop them down to us, and Nibblets can put them in our sacks."

"Miley and I will pick from the lower down bushes," answered Nutmeg.

"Smart thinking," Pinwheel and Hoverine answered in unison. "It will be fun to help."

With that said, the serious business of berry picking began, with one berry for the sacks and one for their tummies.

"Look out below!"

"I found some good juicy ones over here!"

"Watch your head, Nibblets. Here come some more berries down to ya!"

And so their afternoon went.

"Oh, my tummy hurts," groaned Nutmeg.

"I think I'm gonna throw up," answered a very green Miley.

"Look at Nibblets. He looks like he's gonna explode any second," Nutmeg said, looking over at their little friend.

Little Nibblets had indeed expanded in the tummy area. "I can't move," Nibblets said. "I'll be here all winter. I'm gonna turn into a snowball, and nobody will find me."

"I think we should just lie here for awhile and get to feeling better," groaned Nutmeg.

"The way I feel, this could take some time," Miley said.

"That's the truth," Nutmeg answered back.

So the rest of the afternoon was spent wondering how long it was going to take them to feel good enough to go home, and the two dragon-flies pondered the idea of going for help.

Nutmeg

Nibblets

Freefall had caught up with Ebbé, and he liked the winter burrow. He'd met Raindrip, and they had exchanged stories on how they got their names. They took an instant liking to each other and decided they would get along wonderfully.

Raindrip asked Freefall to help keep the winter watch, and Freefall accepted with pride at having been asked. Now Ebbé had two friends to watch fly. And fly they did. Beyond the reach of the two dragonflies, they soared and circled and glided on the invisible staircase. They swooped and played up in their domain, a falcon and an owl becoming best of friends.

Ebbé was so happy for Freefall and happy for their little Nibblets, who also had found new friends. And the dragonflies had each other. But Ebbé began to feel a bit of sadness creep into his heart, because they didn't need him as much as in the beginning of the summer. Freefall was a handsome falcon, all grown up. Nibblets would always need looking after. He was such a sweet little lemming, so trusting. Ebbé thought what he was feeling might be a touch of loneliness for his family. He was far away from home. He decided that, come next spring, he would turn himself about toward his home.

The last few weeks of autumn were spent getting ready for winter and remembering the last of summer's sweetness. Rooka dropped by to say hello. He was looking forward to watching over everyone for another winter. Hoverine and Pinwheel found just about all the berry patches that were to be found.

With the dragonflies leading the way, Nibblets, Nutmeg, and Miley went out picking as many berries as they could put away for winter. And unlike the first time of berry picking, more berries ended up in the knapsacks than in their tummies. Together they also put away a good supply of nuts, so their food gathering was just about done.

Raindrip showed Freefall the boundaries of their patch of the forest and introduced him to the other birds, who protected their own areas. Together all the birds flew together, soaring up into the clear, cold sky, chasing and swooping, making their wings stronger so they would be ready to fly in a storm. "You have to know at all times where you are when you fly in a storm, Freefall," Raindrip said. "There are times when the ground and sky become one, and nothing but shades of gray and white. You have to know where you are for your safety."

Freefall completed his job of gathering pine needles and moss to make beds for everyone, and Ebbé, Marionberry, and Cornflower lined the burrows. They wove mats for their beds and made blankets to keep them warm on the cold winter nights that were just around the corner.

Cornflower

Much to the delight of Marionberry and Cornflower, they were given the task of keeping an eye on Nibblets so none of Nutmeg's or Miley's bad habits would rub off on him. They thought he was the cutest creature in their forest. The small furry group could be seen each afternoon napping in the last rays of the late summer sun.

Fall stepped in and changed the color of the land to rich autumn gold, red, and burnt orange. The evening sky reflected these colors at dusk. The sun, tired of staying up so late through the summer, set earlier with each passing day. She was looking forward to her winter nap.

Nibblets and the younglings had great fun jumping in the piles of colored leaves and playing hide and seek. One afternoon, after a good romp, they lay back to take a rest.

"This was how Ebbé found me last spring," Nibblets said. "I was running and I did a rollover and got covered with leaves. By the time I got myself uncovered and upright, my family was gone."

What did you do then?" asked Marionberry.

Marionberry

"I hid in some bushes with my eyes shut as tight as I could get them. I didn't know what to do, 'cause I was just little at the time. That's when Ebbé and Freefall found me. They've been my family ever since."

"Do you miss your family, or think about them?" asked Cornflower.

"Yes, I do. I always wonder where they are and if they miss me too. When I think about them and feel sad, I think of Ebbé and Freefall and of how lucky I am that they found me. Maybe someday I'll see my family again." Nibblets stopped, heaved a big sigh, and whispered to himself, "Oh, I hope so."

"We hope you do to, Nibblets," said Marionberry. "But you have a new family, and we all love you just the same as your family does."

Cornflower added, "Yeah, Nibblets, you're lucky 'cause you have two families who love you, and lot and lots of friends."

"I love you lots too," answered little Nibblets while pushing a tear off his cheek.

It was a beautiful fall colored day. Freefall was flying over the field, watching Nibblets make his daily circles. Freefall was making loop-de-loops, lost in the golden clouds. He was making one last loop when he happened to see two hawks flying low, circling little Nibblets. Suddenly, one of them swooped little Nibblets up in his talons and flew off.

Freefall's reaction was quick: without thinking, he rolled over and flew after them. He started gaining on them and at the same time wondering what he would do when he caught up to them. He had almost caught up when the hawk released little Nibblets from his talons.

Freefall froze as he watched his little friend fall to earth. He broke off his chase to get to Nibblets but knew he wouldn't make it in time. Just as he had lost hope, Raindrip swooped in and caught Nibblets in his talons. There was just a quick glance between the two friends before Freefall broke off and turned to go after the hawks. With anger in his heart, he flew faster than he ever had.

They didn't see him coming up behind them. His attack was quick as he bumped into one of the hawks, sending him tumbling out of the sky. The other hawk heard the swooping of Freefall's wings and made a sharp turn to his left, with Freefall close behind. The first hawk, after regaining his flight, caught up to Freefall from behind and nudged him with his beak, sending Freefall into a tailspin. But Freefall quickly recovered and did a dragonfly loop-de-loop, circling back around the two hawks. The three birds twisted and turned in the golden evening sky, swooping at each other.

Their squawking filled the air as all the forest friends gathered in the field to watch the birds high up in the sky swoop and chase each other, Freefall against the two hawks. "Look at him go, Ebbé," the two dragonflies said in unison. "He's doing the loops we taught him, and they can't keep up or get away from him." The family of friends watched as Freefall looped and attacked the two hawks and then made another loop and attacked again.

Finally the two birds gave up. Freefall came up beside them and said, "If you ever come back to this forest, I'll be waiting, and you'll be sorry you did. Now go!"

The hawks nodded out of respect to Freefall. The larger hawk said, "We've lived in this forest a long time and have never seen a bird fly like you. We'll leave this airspace to you but hope someday to have the honor of flying by your side as friends." They again nodded and flew out of the airspace that came to be known throughout all the forests as the sky that belongs to the falcon that flies like a dragonfly.

The forest friends watched as Freefall became silhouetted against the gold and red sunset, flying high up in the evening sky, doing his loop-de-loops dragonfly style. All the friends and forest creatures knew they would be safe with Freefall and Raindrip to look after them.

⊲⊂⊙⊃⊳

The green of summer had slipped into the gold of autumn then faded into the gray of winter. They spent the last few good days making sure everything was ready when winter would cover their world in a blanket of white.

One evening, Freefall made an announcement after everyone had gathered for their before-bedtime visit. "Raindrip has asked me to nest up with him for the winter. That way we can both keep a better eye out for danger. Is that okay with you, Ebbé?"

Ebbé felt a lump in this throat, but swallowed it back down before answering, "Oh, Freefall, what a good idea."

"We'll certainly be safe with Freefall, Raindrip, and Rooka watching over us, huh, Ebbé," said a tired Nibblets.

"Yes, you're right, Nibblets. We're all very lucky to have each other. But, I think, by the looks of you, it's time to turn in for the night." So with that, they said their good-nights to each other, entered their burrows, and cozied up under their Ebbé blankets, each to their own sweet dreams.

⊲⊂⊙⊃⊳

The next few weeks brought colder and colder weather. The sky turned a darker shade of gray and threatened snow. They found themselves out less and less. Instead, they would gather in Ebbé's burrow, since it was big enough to hold all of them.

They talked about the idea of wintering together in Ebbé's burrow and using Mrs. Latchshaw's for food storage. They discussed this over a period of nights for lack of anything else important to discuss. It was finally agreed that they would give it a try but that the younglings must behave themselves and not cause too much ruckus. If they did, Mrs. Latchshaw and her younglings would be asked to 'please' go back to their own burrow. With lots of "Oh, we promise we won't fight. We'll be good."

"Oh please can we winter together!" It was settled; they were now one extra-large family.

Ebbé had quietly spent some secret time alone. He had found a place in the woods and carved some games and toys for Nibblets and the four rabbits. They were like the toys Ebbé had played with when he was a youngling.

With great delight and big happy smiles, the gifts were exchanged. To Ebbe's surprise Marionberry and cornflower had made him a new warm cape. The younglings had fun playing with the toys and Ebbe strutted around showing off his new cape. The younglings had fun playing with the toys, and Ebbé strutted around, showing off his new cape.

Most nights, Freefall and Raindrip whiled away the evenings with them. Sometimes the two birds made their rounds together, giving them a chance for some fly time. Other times they took turns at the watch. They always came back with news about what was going on in the other parts of the forest. This way all the creatures stayed in touch, warning each other of danger and sharing happy news.

There were always funny stories to report, like the time Stooky and Smack, two resident raccoons, got Callalily, one of the resident skunks, mad at them. "Has anyone told you that you certainly don't smell as nice as your name?" Stooky said one day to Callalily. Everyone knew this was a bad idea. You never say anything to skunks about the way they smell, and especially not a girl skunk. Poor Stooky spent the next day in the pond, trying to get himself smelling better. He spent the next week listening to all his friends tease him. "Hey, Stooky, you smell as pretty as Callalily!"

And of course everyone knew the story of when Nutmeg and Miley got poor little Nibblets so sick on berries they thought he would explode, and they had to bundle him up in a knapsack and have Rooka carry him home. Nibblets lay for hours, looking like he'd eaten their winter's supply of berries. They didn't think his tummy would ever get back to its normal size. But it did, and Nibblets decided, just maybe, he didn't like that kind of berry as much as he thought.

The snow started falling a few weeks later, but it didn't keep the younglings from going outside to run off their extra energy. Rooka and Ebbé shook the tree limbs so all the snow fell on the youngling's heads. They saw which younglings could dig themselves out the fastest. Nibblets was the better digger and most times won, with Cornflower coming in a close second.

There were still berries left in some of the patches. Sometimes the younglings would gather up their knapsacks and go berry picking, always in a group of two, so no one was alone. They were still too young to venture out by themselves.

As more and more snow piled up, a strange and magical thing started happening to Nibblets. He began to turn white. One night, after the evening meal, Nutmeg asked Ebbé about this.

"Nibblets is turning white for his protection," explained Ebbé. "This has happened to lemmings for generations, according to a very old legend passed down through time. These tiny, pure-white creatures can be seen gently falling to earth, always descending in a spiral during snowstorms." Everyone looked at their Nibblets with awe. "Nibblets," Ebbé said, "you truly are our special little friend."

The first bad snow hit on the third of December. Freefall and Raindrip were scouting to see what they could see and find out what needed to be found out. Both left in different directions, and both came back quickly, bearing the same bad news. "Got a storm moving in fast, Ebbé," said Freefall.

The tallest trees looked out for weather changes that could bring flood, fire, or blizzard, anything that posed a threat to all creatures of the forests and meadows. There was one posted in each corner of the forest. This honor was given to the tallest, strongest, and wisest trees.

Freefall had gone to speak to the North Tree and the East Tree, while Raindrip had gone to the South Tree and the West Tree. Freefall reported, "The North and East Trees both see a very bad storm on the horizon. It's com'n' in fast and dark."

Just then, Raindrip flew down and landed by Freefall. "Good, you've already carried the news back, Freefall. Even though it's going to hit hardest here in the North Forest, first warnings are going out as far as the South Forest for all to prepare. Looks like it will be the worst of storms. It's like none we've ever seen before, heading our way." With that said, Freefall and Raindrip went out to find Rooka so he could gather birds to send out the warning.

Ebbé gathered his small family to start making plans. "Mrs. Latchshaw, you and the younglings start carrying the supplies over from your burrow to our burrow. We should have it in with us because, as sure as I'm standing here, we're going to get snowed in. We don't want anyone out in the storm. Be careful, all of you, and make sure you listen to your mama. Mrs. Latchshaw, please be careful, and if it looks like the weather is turning, come back here right away."

Ebbé turned to the dragonflies and said, "Hoverine and Pinwheel, go check on everyone in our area to make sure they all get the news so they can put their plans into action. If anyone needs anything or any help, come back and get me." Off the dragonflies went to carry the news to the others.

"Mrs. Latchshaw, I'm going to make sure our burrow is safe and sound and then get that extra area ready to store all our supplies in." Ebbé clapped his hands together and said, "Let's get going!"

Off everyone went, each with his own task to do and his or her own thoughts of how this would all end up. This was not the future Ebbé had in mind for himself or his friends. It would be a long, tiring night for everyone.

"Nibblets, keep making noises, 'cause I'm losing you in the snow," said Cornflower. Nibblets took a deep breath and said, "I'll try to remember, but I keep forgetting, 'cause I'm trying to remember so many things that I'm getting confused. I haven't been confused for the longest time!"

"It's okay," Cornflower said, trying her best to reassure Nibblets. "Just take another deep breath. I'll keep my eyes on you. You'll be just fine."

"Oh, I hope so, 'cause I'm scared."

"After the storm goes through, you'll see."

Ebbé had gotten the burrow ready for everyone and put the food into the new storage area that Mrs. Latchshaw and the younglings had brought over. It would be crowded but would certainly be warm with everyone cozied up together.

Mrs. Latchshaw and the younglings were making one more trip for the last of the supplies. The wind had picked up, and the temperature was dropping fast. It was time to finish their tasks and gather everyone in. Freefall and Raindrip would be staying in the burrow with them, and Rooka would stay just outside the entrance.

Freefall landed next to Ebbé and gave his wings a good shake. "Everyone seems to be doing okay, Ebbé."

Raindrip landed by them. "It's getting cold out here, and the snow is starting to come down heavy," he said, shaking the snow off himself. "Where are Mrs. Latchshaw and the younglings, Ebbé? We need to get everybody gathered up and into the burrow. I think our time has run out."

"I'm getting very concerned about them," Ebbé said, cupping his hands over his eyes to keep the snow out. They should have been back by now."

No sooner had Ebbé gotten the words out of his mouth than Pinwheel and Hoverine came sputtering down to the ground. "Snow's gettin' too heavy for us to fly," they said together. "We hurried back to let you know we've got trouble! We can't find Nibblets! Mrs. Latchshaw said they turned around for a second, and he was gone. We've been looking everywhere, but he's nowhere to be found."

Ebbé felt like he couldn't breathe. The thought of something happening to Nibblets was unthinkable to him. "Quick, Freefall and Raindrip, let's go help them search."

"I'm going to stay here in case they make it back, Ebbé. You and Freefall go," answered Raindrip as he felt a chill crawl up his spine.

They left in the direction of Mrs. Latchshaw's burrow. The snow was coming down heavy; it was now a whiteout. They couldn't see anything beyond two feet in front of them, at best.

"Keep together," Ebbé yelled over the wind to Freefall. "Stay right behind me." He was afraid they might get lost, even if they did find Nibblets. He and Freefall kept trying to go forward, but the wind was picking up speed and spitting snow in their eyes. For every two steps forward, the wind pushed them back one. It was as if they were walking into the mouth of a great roaring beast.

"Are you okay behind me, Freefall?"

"Yes, Ebbé, and I think I see a shadow coming this way, over to you left."

Just then Rooka showed up and yelled, "Here, walk under me. I can keep some of this wind and snow off you. I've never seen a storm this strong before!" They couldn't see anything at all through the blinding snow.

"Freefall," yelled Ebbé, "look over to you right. I think I see them."

The wet, snow-covered group was huddled together under a snow-laden pine. "Oh, Ebbé! I don't know what happened," cried Mrs. Latchshaw. "One second he was here, and the next he wasn't. I feel awful, just awful. We've looked high and low, under every tree and bush, but we can't find him. He simply vanished."

"It'll be okay," Ebbé said, trying his best to comfort her. "Rooka, take them back to the burrow." Ebbé turned to Mrs. Latchshaw and yelled, "You and the younglings get under Rooka for shelter, and he'll take you back. You need to get yourselves dry and warm. Tell Raindrip that Freefall and I are going to keep looking. We'll find him." But Ebbé had never been so scared.

His violent rolling had finally come to a stop. Nibblets lay still for a minute, wondering what he should do. He had his eyes tightly shut for fear of what he would see. He slowly opened them, but even with them opened a little bit, he saw nothing. He closed his eyes and then slowly reopened them just enough to see something—anything. But his world was totally black. He closed his eyes again and wished his Ebbé was there with him, but he knew he was alone.

Nibblets began to feel a sharp pain in his front leg. He didn't know where he was, but he knew he had to find a way out of that scary, dark place. He didn't know which way was up or which way was down, so he couldn't tell in what direction to start digging. He realized he was jammed so tightly in the snow, he could barely move. Beyond the pain he felt in his leg was the fear of never seeing his friends again, and that hurt too much to think about. Nibblets knew he had to dig himself out. If only he knew where to start.

"Oh please, pretty forest faerie. Please, Ebbé, please help me!" Nibblets cried.

Nibblets lay very still and tried not to let the panic he was feeling take over. His leg hurt even more than he thought possible. He wouldn't give up. They had to find him; he'd be okay. For now, he just wanted to sleep.

✧

Everyone else had gotten back to Ebbé's burrow safe and sound, though very cold and wet. Freefall and Raindrip couldn't fly in the storm; it would be crazy to try. They could easily get hurt or lost.

Rooka was lying down outside the entrance to the burrow. Ebbé looked at Rooka and said, "Rooka, will your brothers help us find Nibblets?"

"I'll go back to the place Nibblets was last seen and have a good sniff around. And I'll put out a call to my brothers. We'll dig around the area to see if we can find him. This storm will have to settle down though, before we can search."

"I know; it's going to be hard to wait, but I know," answered Ebbé.

"I feel so helpless," Mrs. Latchshaw said. "We just turned around, and he was gone. It's my fault that he's missing. Oh, Ebbé, I'm so sorry." With that, she covered her face and started crying. Her younglings went over to their mama and cuddled up close to her. "Ma," Marionberry said between sobs, "it's my fault. I said I'd keep an eye on him, and I let him down."

"No, my little one, you didn't let him down. It's just something that happened. We all kept losing him in the deep snow. Please, my dear sweet younglings, no one blames any of you." She snuggled them close to her. "Let's say a pray to the protector of all creatures to keep our Nibblets safe in his arms until he is back with us."

In silence they closed their eyes and bowed their heads, and each offered a prayer from their heart to protect their sweet friend and bring him home to them.

"We promise," said Marionberry between sobs, "we'll never let him out of our site again, ever."

"And I promise," Miley said, "that I'll never let him sick on berries again." And so for the longest time a small group of friends that had become a family huddled together while offering prayers and giving promises for Nibblets. Outside their burrow, the storm raged on.

✺

Nibblets woke again. Nothing had changed in his world; it was still as black as endless time. The pain in his leg was becoming unbearable. He knew he had to start digging himself out but didn't know if he could with his leg. He had to try to save himself. He braced himself with his back legs while trying to turn his body around to position his good leg so he could use it to start digging. He still didn't know in which direction to start.

"Oh, Ebbé, please help me to know the right way to start," Nibblets said aloud. "Please help me get back to my friends." After taking a deep breath, he began to dig at the snow, but he found there was no place to put the snow he was digging. It was packed around his body so tightly that he had no room to move.

Still not sure of which direction to go, he knew it would be better to go anywhere than feel helplessly trapped where he was. Taking a deep breath, he began.

◖◉ ◉◗

Rooka and his brothers came upon the area where Nibblets had last been seen. "This is where he was lost," said Rooka. "Buckley, sniff around the pine over there. That's Mrs. Latchshaw's burrow. Maybe you can pick up a scent. Vic, you sniff over in that area. That's the path back to Ebbé's burrow. It's a small area, but with the snow so deep and Nibblets so tiny, there is a lot of area for us to cover. I'm going to sniff around here, just in case they got off the path in the blizzard and started heading back in the wrong direction. Dig carefully, and if you pick up a scent, call out."

With that the three bucks, in the middle of the worst blizzard that anyone could remember, began their search. As hard as they tried, they couldn't pick up a scent, and they were left to wait out the storm with the others.

It seemed like forever before the storm gave any signs of letting up. The entrance to Ebbé's burrow was buried deep in snow, so Rooka started digging to get to his friends. The group emerged to a world of quiet white.

It was early morning. The sun cast a soft pink glow over the snow-covered forest. All was calm in the forest as snow lightly drifted down. Slowly they heard the sounds of other creatures as one by one they started to appear from their burrows. They all knew about Nibblets and looked silently over at Ebbé's family. "Any luck?" asked one of the neighbors. Seeing the look on their faces said it all. Nibblets was still missing.

"We're all here to help you search, Ebbé," the neighbor said.

(( ))

Nibblets started digging again. After what seemed like days, he found himself in a small hollow of an old, burned-out pine. He didn't know where he was, since so much snow covered the ground. He was tired from digging, but happy to have found a small cubby to sleep in. His leg was still extremely painful. He needed to rest, so he closed his eyes to sleep, but all he could do was cry.

(( ))

The day was filled with mixed emotions for all who lived in the North Forest. The word of Nibblets's disappearance spread throughout all the corners of the forest, and soon the forest was a beehive of activity.

Ebbé tried his best to keep order, but there were so many helpers and so much on his mind. "Ebbé," Rooka said, "let me take over and organize the search for you."

"Thanks," Ebbé replied. "I've got so much to think about, I can't keep a straight thought. But I need to keep busy doing something."

"Have a talk with Mrs. Latchshaw to find out all you can, so we can retrace the path they took."

"That's a good idea. Thanks, Rooka." Ebbé walked over to Mrs. Latchshaw, and they tried their best to figure out what direction they had gone. "The snow was coming down so heavy when we left the burrow that I'm not sure which way we started back," she said. "We may have started off in the wrong direction. Oh, land's sakes, I wish I could remember. I was so busy gathering up the younglings that I didn't notice."

"Please don't cry, mama. We'll find him," said Cornflower.

"We have lots of help," Ebbé said. "It's going to be okay; you'll see."

"Oh, I hope so. I just don't think I could bare it if Nibblets isn't found."

"Don't say that, mama. We'll find him," cried Miley.

The day went slowly in some ways and too quickly in other ways. The forest was combed over, and holes appeared in the snow everywhere. Nightfall was upon them, and everyone was tired and cold. They decided it would be best if everyone they went to their burrows for a good night's sleep. They would start fresh at daybreak.

"Ebbé," Raindrip said, "I know Nibblets will be found."

"I hope you're right. I've got to think positive about this. Thanks for saying that to me. I need to hear some good things right now." Ebbé entered his burrow for a long, sleepless night while Rooka guarded the entrance.

The next morning, dark clouds began to gather over the forest. Raindrip had gotten back from visiting with all four of the forest trees, and he reported, "The West Tree says another storm is heading our way, but it won't be as bad as this last one." Raindrip had gotten back from visiting with all four of the forest trees.

By late morning, snow began to fall again. Nibblets had been missing three days, and Ebbé was beginning to fear the worst. And now another storm was moving in. He knew time was running out.

"I don't know what to do, Ebbé," said a frustrated Freefall. "I feel utterly helpless."

(( ))

Nibblets was cold and hungry, and he was having a hard time staying awake. He didn't have any fight left in him. He dreamed of summer and running in the meadows, learning to run so he wouldn't do rollovers. He remembered watching Freefall learn to fly, and Pinwheel and Hoverine teaching him all about loop-de-loops dragonfly style.

He could taste the wild berries that he'd picked with Nutmeg and Miley, and feel the cozy evenings spent in Ebbé's burrow. There had been so many happy times in his life.

He found himself sleeping more while slipping into his world of memories. He remembered Ebbé telling him all about his family, how they came down to earth when it snowed. In his dreams, he pictured them in his mind. They were coming for him. He would be so happy to meet them. They would ask him to go home with them to their beautiful world of glistening snow.

(( ))

"Look over there in the sky. Do you see that?" asked Mrs. Latchshaw. "Look, Ebbé, what is that?"

Ebbé looked over to where she was pointing and stared. All the creatures stopped what they were doing and looked to where she was pointing.

As the snow swirled down in a spiral, tiny, pure-white lemmings were intermixed among the snowflakes, slowly making their way to earth.

They all knew this had something to do with Nibblets. The lemmings silently landed. Just as they touched the ground, they disappeared into the snow, right where Nibblets had been lost.

"They've found Nibblets! I know it," Ebbé said. Then he held his breath, not knowing if this was a good or a bad thing. No one moved, and they hardly breathed. The forest lay very calm and strangely silent.

❪◖ ◗❫

Nibblets had a feeling he wasn't alone. He didn't hurt anymore, and there was warmth surrounding him. He thought he should open his eyes. He thought just maybe it had all been a bad dream and he was really home, safe in Ebbé's burrow after all.

"Nibblets," said a soft, beautiful voice. "Nibblets, we've come for you. You are safe with us now. Wake up, Nibblets. We're your family, and we've come to take you home."

Nibblets thought, *What a pretty voice. I know I've heard it before.* He felt so peaceful that he didn't know whether he wanted to open his eyes to see who the voice belonged to or just sleep and keep dreaming. Then he thought the pretty voice sounded just like the forest faerie, and maybe she was there with him. He thought he should open his eyes and see.

"Nibblets, wake up. It's time to go home with us," the voice softly said again. Nibblets decided it was time to see. He opened his eyes very slowly. They felt heavy, so he had to work to open them. He found himself looking into the faces of beautiful, pure-white lemmings—and into his mama's eyes.

"Hello, my little Nibblets," said Snowberry. "We have come to take you home, my little one." Nibblets looked at her and closed his eyes.

Hoping she would still be there, he opened his eyes again. She was still there, smiling at him. And Nibblets smiled at Snowberry, his mama.

It seemed like forever since the lemmings had vanished into the snow. Nobody moved. They just waited. Then, as magically as they had disappeared into the snow, they reappeared, and Nibblets was with them. They had found Nibblets.

Ebbé stepped away from the group and walked over to the lemmings. He smiled at them. Snowberry smiled at Ebbé and said, "I am Snowberry, Nibblets's mama, and this is his family." She tucked little Nibblets close to her body, smiled at Ebbé, and said, "You found our Nibblets when he was lost. We don't have the words to express our feelings. He told us how you took care of him, Ebbé, and how you loved and nurtured him." Snowberry looked at little Nibblets by her side. "We thought he was lost to us forever, but you've given him back to us Ebbé."

Snowberry saw the love in Ebbé's eyes when he looked at Nibblets, her baby. The other lemmings gathered around Nibblets and his mama, as if protecting them, but when Ebbé smiled at them, they smiled back, knowing there was nothing to fear.

"It is time for Nibblets to learn about his past so he can know his future. Please understand, Ebbé. This has been our way since the beginning of time and will always be until the end of time in our realm. You have loved and cared for him since that day, and we thank you for the gift of love you gave him. Nibblets will always be with you in your heart, as you will be in his. Someday you will see Nibblets again Ebbé. This I promise you."

Ebbé felt a deep pain in his heart, and he knew he was helpless to change the future. He wanted to go back to when life had been simple and full of long sunny days. He remembered what the faerie and the guide

Mommy and Nibblets

disguised as a tree had told him: "Sometimes we can choose our future, and sometimes our future chooses us."

He guessed this was true for all of earth's creatures, even little Nibblets. Ebbé had thought that part of his future would always be to look after Nibblets, who was so sweet and needed to be cared for. Now he knew this was not to be.

Snowberry said, "Our futures are linked with another's future as a continuous chain linked one to another."

And so the time had come for Ebbé to pass on the "looking after" of Nibblets to Snowberry and her family. This was Nibblet's future.

It was heartbreaking for Nibblets's friends and family for they had all become a family to say good-bye to him. "We love you, Nibblets. I'm going to miss you so much," Marionberry said as she hugged her little friend good-bye.

"Now, don't go eating too many berries so you get sick," said Miley as he patted Nibblets on his head.

"Be cool, Nibblets. I'll miss you lots," Nutmeg said, holding back his tears.

"I love you, little Nibblets, but I'm glad your family found you," Cornflower said as she kissed him on the top of his head.

"You've been just like one of my own younglings," Mrs. Latchshaw said as she just about squeezed the air out of him.

"It's been my pleasure knowing you, Nibblets," Rooka said as he swallowed down the lump in his throat.

"Seems like your family and future have come for you, little one," Raindrip said.

"We'll keep teaching Freefall new flying tricks, Nibblets," Pinwheel and Hoverine said in unison.

Freefall stepped up to Nibblets and touched his nose with his feathered wing tip. "You will always travel in my heart," he whispered.

And then it was Ebbé's turn to say good-bye. He picked up his Nibblets and held him close to his heart, doing his best to put his feeling to memory. "My little friend, I'm going to miss you so much, but I'm happy that your family has found you. I hope the time is short between our good-bye and our hello."

"I love you so much, Ebbé," Nibblets said, brushing a tear off Ebbé's cheek. He looked at everyone and smiled. "I'm gonna miss you guys. I love you lots." And then little Nibblets curled up in Ebbé's arms, wishing Ebbé could go with him. But he knew in his heart that Ebbé's future was taking him on another path. Nibblets looked at his Ebbé and whispered, "I hope you find your brightly wrapped present, Ebbé."

It was dusk in the forest. Nibblets and the lemmings began to glow, just like the forest faerie when she had left. Maybe, just maybe, Nibblets's future was going to be something special after all. But the future was tomorrow, and now was the time for good-bye.

Surrounded by a million twinkling lights, just like when the lemmings had arrived, they vanished, leaving behind a trail of shimmering dust.

That night, Ebbé decided it was time for him to go home. He missed his family. His two little friends had grown up. Freefall had found a home in the North Forest with Raindrip, and little Nibblets was tucked away with his family in their realm of winter white.

Come spring, Ebbé would journey home, but for now he turned over and dreamed of all the memories he would always hold close to his heart. And he wondered what his brightly wrapped present would be.

Printed in the United States
By Bookmasters